A Decision Is Yours Book

UNDER WHOSE INFLUENCE?

By Judy Laik

Illustrated by
Rebekah J. Strecker

LC 93-086233
ISBN 0-943990-97-1 Paperback
ISBN 0-943990-98-X Library binding

Parenting Press, Inc.
P.O. Box 75267
Seattle, WA 98125

http://www.ParentingPress.com

BEFORE YOU BEGIN

Most books you read tell you about other people's decisions.

This book is different! *You* make the decisions. *You* decide what happens next.

Have you ever made a decision and found things didn't turn out the way you'd planned? It happens all the time. Did you ever dream about going back and trying again? What would have happened if you had done something differently?

In this book you'll find out how it feels when you are pressured to drink alcohol. You'll have lots of chances to choose different ways of acting. You make the decisions. Good luck!

Turn the page and see what happens.

NAPA VALLEY UNIFIED SCHOOL DISTRICT
ELEMENTARY COUNSELING PROGRAM

The school bus roars away, belching exhaust. You **1** are going to your classmate Nicole's house to work on a science project with her and her friend Katherine. You feel a little shy—you don't know these girls very well.

As you approach Nicole's house, you hear loud music. "That's my sister Michelle," Nicole says. "She won't bother us. She's always on the phone."

Nicole says, "Let's eat before we start working on the electrical generator."

In the kitchen, she puts a frozen pizza in the oven. Then she opens a high cupboard. "Look!"

You see bottles of different colors and shapes. The labels read "whiskey," "vodka," and other kinds of alcohol.

"Uh, we'd better not drink that," says Katherine.

"We can't," you say. "Those are your parents'."

"They don't mind. My mom even told me to offer my friends anything they want." Nicole takes down a bottle of whiskey. "I want to try it."

Nicole looks at you. "Are you guys in or out?"

Katherine looks worried. "I guess it would be fun." She gets three glasses.

You know you will all get in trouble if you drink whiskey. Just thinking about it makes you feel sick.

If you decide not to drink, turn to page 3.
If you decide to try the whiskey, turn to page 5.

"I'd rather have soda," you say. **3**

"Don't be a chicken, Jamie," says Nicole as she pours whiskey into two glasses.

Katherine gets a cola out of the refrigerator. "Mix this with the whiskey," she says to you.

"No, rum," says Nicole. "Haven't you heard of 'rum-and-cola'?" She takes down another bottle.

You *are* scared, but you don't want Nicole and Katherine to know. "If we get bombed, we won't get the science project done. My mother would kill me."

"Baby Jamie! Can't have any fun because her mommy will get mad!" laughs Nicole.

"Your mother won't know if you don't tell her." Katherine adds.

You want to be friends with Nicole and Katherine. If you refuse to drink, they might not like you. But you know your mother will be upset if you drink.

If you decide to drink, turn to page 5.
If you want to stay friends with Nicole and Katherine without drinking, turn to page 7.

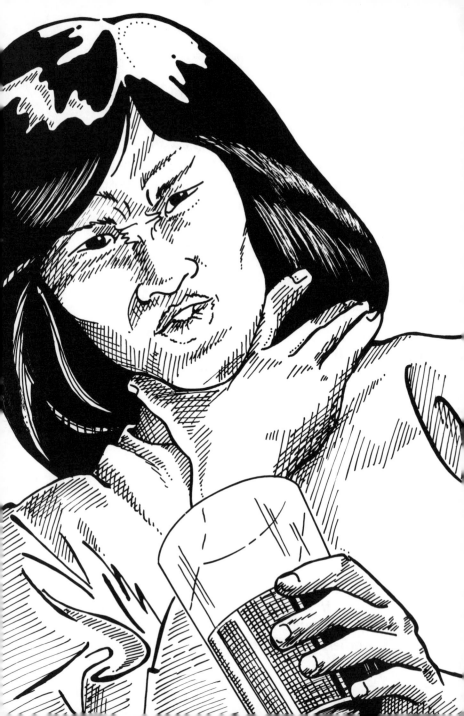

You say, "Just a little." **5**

"Want whiskey, or rum-and-cola?" asks Nicole.

"I'll drink what you're having." You all clink glasses together just like in the movies.

"Cheers!" Katherine gulps down her drink and chokes. Her eyes stream and her face turns red.

Nicole sips hers. You watch. Your stomach tightens into a hard ball.

After Katherine stops choking, both girls wait for you.

"Here goes." You take a tiny sip. The sour taste makes your face pucker up. The whiskey burns your throat. You put your glass down. "Let's have soda with the pizza."

"No, vodka," says Nicole. "I've heard it doesn't have any taste. Maybe it's not as bad as whiskey."

If you decide to stop, turn to page 9.
If you keep on drinking, turn to page 11.

"Go ahead and drink if you want. I've tried it   **7** before and I don't like the taste. I'll just have soda," you say. You pour cola into the third glass.

"It isn't fun if we don't all do it," says Nicole.

You don't know what to do. You won't drink, but you don't want to be enemies. You wish you could go home. It's a long way to walk, and you'd have to cross a busy highway.

If you call your mother to come get you, she'll ask why. Nicole's father, Mr. Beller, was supposed to drive you when he got home. If you tell your mother what's happening, she will probably tell the girls' parents.

If you walk home, you could pretend to your mother that everything was normal.

Or you could stay at Nicole's house and just not drink.

If you stay at Nicole's, turn to page 13.
If you call your mother, turn to page 15.
If you walk home, turn to page 19.

You hate how alcohol tastes and you decide not to drink anymore. Nicole's sister Michelle is still in her room. You wish she would stop the girls.

You go into the family room and start on your homework. You decide how to make your electrical generator and list the parts you need.

Nicole and Katherine giggle and clink glasses in the kitchen. Later, they stumble into the family room. Katherine falls down, and Nicole collapses on top of her. They both laugh so hard they can't get back up.

Then Nicole says, "Let's call up numbers in the phone book. I heard this joke. You call a number and ask if there are any Walls there. When they say no, you ask, 'Well, then what's holding up your ceiling?'"

Katherine and Nicole dial numbers at random. They laugh loudly. You think it's dumb, but don't say anything. They're too drunk to listen, anyway.

When Nicole's parents get home, the girls act quiet. The Bellers don't notice anything wrong, although Katherine's face is pale.

"Let's work on our assignment again tomorrow," Nicole says. You wish you didn't have to work on the project with them.

If you decide to finish the science project with them, turn to page 21.
If you want to stop working with them, turn to page 23.

Nicole pours vodka into your glass. You take a sip. *Whew!* Vodka *does* have a taste—it tastes like the rubbing alcohol your mother uses to clean the fever thermometer!

"Let's mix it with soda." Nicole pours cola into each glass. You can still taste the alcohol, but it isn't as bad.

After you finish the glass your head spins. Nicole and Katherine are acting silly; their noise and Michelle's loud music seem to crash in your head.

If you are going to stop drinking, turn to page 25.
If you don't tell the girls you want to stop,
turn to page 29.

"Go ahead if you want to," you say. "I want to get a good grade on the project. I'll just have soda."

Although the girls look at you like you're trying to spoil their fun, they drop the subject.

The oven timer buzzes. You all take the food and drinks into the family room. You eat pizza with them. They get some more whiskey. They giggle and act like they have some big secret.

They won't talk to you, and you feel rejected. You almost wish you had agreed to drink with them. Maybe if you did, they would accept you as a friend.

If you decide you can still drink, turn to page 47.
If you decide not to, turn to page 53.

You're worried about what your mother will say. **15** But you feel uncomfortable staying at Nicole's house. The oven buzzes. Nicole takes the pizza into the family room.

You say, "Just a minute," and pretend to get a drink of water.

You dial home. "Mom, could you come get me?"

By the time she arrives, Nicole and Katherine are throwing olive and pepperoni slices around the family room. You rush out and jump in the car. Your mother gives you her "explanation time" look.

"Nicole and Katherine were drinking alcohol," you say. "I didn't want to."

"I'm glad you called me, Jamie. I know it wasn't easy to tell me. But I'm worried about those girls drinking. Where's Nicole's sister?"

"She was upstairs talking on the phone. I never saw her."

"What about the girls' parents?"

"The Bellers were both at work. I don't know about Katherine's mother."

"When we get home, I'll try calling Nicole's house and see if her sister is off the phone yet. If not, I'll try to get in touch with the girl's parents."

"Mom, please don't do that! They'll be so mad at me for telling on them."

"I understand it will embarrass you. But the girls can't handle this on their own.

Turn to page 17.

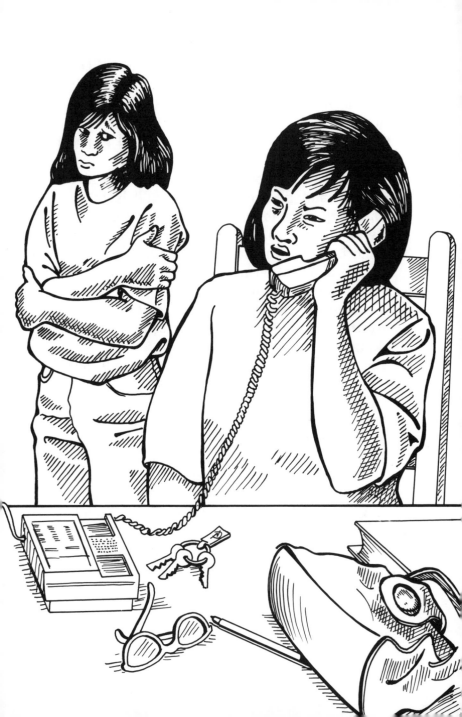

"You would feel much worse if we didn't take some action and one of the girls became seriously ill."

You nod. "I guess. But I don't think they'll understand."

When you get home, your mother reaches Mr. Beller at the Bellers' store.

Your mother says, "It *is* my business. My own daughter's safety was involved. If something happened to one of the girls, you could get sued. I don't think you'd want that."

When she gets off the phone, she tells you that Mr. Beller is going to check on the girls. Later, she reaches Katherine's mother, but finds that the Bellers have already told her.

Your mother goes to school the next day and discusses the science project with your teacher. Mr. Burke assigns you a different project that you can do on your own.

Katherine and Nicole won't talk to you. You feel bad about that. But mostly you're relieved that you won't have to go to Nicole's house again.

The End

If you call your mother, Nicole and Katherine might get in trouble and blame you. But you feel uncomfortable staying at Nicole's house. Nicole and Katherine decide to eat the pizza in the family room.

They call you to join them, but you go in the bathroom to think. Your mother has told you drinking is dangerous for kids. You leave the bathroom quietly, put your jacket on, and leave.

You feel relieved as you walk away from the house. By the time you get home it's dark. Your mother says, "I didn't see Mr. Beller's car headlights."

You lie, "He dropped me off at the end of the block. He had to hurry home for dinner."

The next day, Nicole asks, "Where did you go yesterday?" You tell her you walked home.

She says, "Did you hear Katherine is in the hospital? She got alcohol poisoning. She passed out. I thought she was just sleeping. When my parents came home, they couldn't wake her up. I had to tell them we'd been drinking.

"They called her mom, and an ambulance took her to the hospital. She almost died. I didn't know alcohol was so bad for you, or that it could hurt you so quickly. I'll never drink again!"

You feel terrible about Katherine and hope she'll be all right. You think you should have called your mother yesterday.

The End

You feel you have to keep on working with the **21** girls. It would be too embarrassing to explain why you didn't want to.

"Let's meet at my house tomorrow," you say. "It's just a little walk from school." You know your mother will be home. The girls look serious. You bet they wish they hadn't been drinking.

The next day Katherine is absent from school. Nicole explains she got sick from drinking. Nicole doesn't feel well, either. She says they are going to have to postpone the project. "I'll never drink again."

After school, your mother asks why Nicole and Katherine didn't come home with you. "They have the flu," you say. You feel funny lying to her. You work on the science project, but it's hard to do it alone.

The next day, both the girls come to your house. They act embarrassed. The science project gets finished, and you're glad it's all over. You don't have to pretend to be friends any more.

The End

You don't want to do the science project with **23** them. But you don't want to say so with Nicole's parents present. You say, "Okay," and Mr. Beller drives you home.

That evening after dinner, you go out to the garage where Maisie, your basset hound, sleeps. You stroke her silky ears. "What should I do, Maisie?

"I'd rather do my own project. I saw directions to make a simple computer in my book.

"I can't tell Mom or Dad, or Nicole and Katherine will call me a narc. Maybe I could tell Steve. He's mean sometimes, but he's okay for a big brother.

"Or maybe I could talk to our teacher. If I tell him I can't work with Nicole and Katherine without explaining why, he might let me do a project all alone."

Maisie doesn't have any advice. But her brown eyes look sympathetic.

If you decide to ask Steve what to do,
turn to page 35.
If you decide to talk to your teacher,
turn to page 37.

You feel dizzy and sick. You go into the family **25** room and topple onto the sofa.

Nicole asks, "What's the matter, Jamie?" and Katherine says, "She's a baby. Needs a nap!"

You decide you don't like Katherine. "Go away," you mutter.

Nicole says, "Let's go up to my room." Giggling, the two girls leave. Somehow, even though Michelle's music shakes the house, you fall asleep.

A scream awakens you. You sit up groggily, hearing a buzzing noise—the smoke alarm.

"Where's Nicole?" Michelle shouts. "She went to her room with Katherine," you say.

Michelle yells from the bottom of the stairs, "Nicole! You left the pizza in the oven. There's smoke all over! I thought you kids could look after yourselves. Were you drinking? There's whiskey on the counter."

Nicole hangs her head. "We just tried a little."

"I can't believe this!" moans Michelle.

Nicole's eyes tear over. "We'll clean up the mess. Don't tell."

"I'm not letting you out of my sight from now on!" exclaims Michelle.

Everybody works to clean the kitchen. When Mr. and Mrs. Beller come home, they remark on the smoke smell. Michelle tells them about the burnt pizza. No one mentions the alcohol. You're scared that they will still find out.

Turn to page 27.

Nicole and Katherine talk about meeting at the Bellers' the next afternoon to work on the science project.

You don't want to work with them. But if you say so, the Bellers might realize something is wrong. You keep quiet.

The next day, you ride the bus to Nicole's house again. You don't know what to expect. You felt sick to your stomach last night. Nicole and Katherine were even sicker. Katherine missed school today. But she comes over to Nicole's house after you get there.

Michelle stays with all of you and doesn't even play her music. She serves you a snack while you plan your project. Michelle adds some good ideas. You work hard on the assignment that day and the next.

You turn the project in on Monday, and you all get a B+.

On Thursday, your mother is stern-faced when you get home from school. "Mrs. Beller called me today. She noticed that there was liquor missing. When she talked to her girls about it, they admitted Nicole, Katherine, and you had been drinking. I'm very disappointed in you, Jamie."

This is worse than anything you could have imagined.

Turn to page 45.

The oven buzzer sounds. Nicole suggests drinking rum-and-cola with the pizza. You all try that. It tastes kind of funny, but not too bad. You and the girls eat the rest of the pizza. Everything looks hazy. Your head feels dizzy.

Nicole dances to Michelle's music. Everybody laughs. You all dance into the living room with your drinks.

Katherine wobbles, spilling her drink on the white carpet. Everyone laughs at the brown puddle. You stagger into a glass case containing vases and figurines. The door shatters. Several of the pieces go flying. A vase and two figurines break.

"Oh, no," Nicole screams. "My mother will kill me. That stuff is expensive."

You are all shocked into feeling sober. You reach to pick up the broken vase. "Don't touch anything!" Nicole yells. "You'll only break things worse."

Nicole looks scared. You feel scared, too. She says, "Let's clean up the mess in here anyway." You all work together to clean up the carpet and the kitchen. No one wants to work on the science project.

Nicole says, "I'd better tell Michelle what happened. My parents will be mad at her, too, because she was supposed to watch us." She goes upstairs. The music stops. You hear Michelle shrieking.

Turn to page 31.

They come downstairs. Nicole is crying.

"Geez, how could you play in the living room? You and I will be grounded for the rest of our lives," says Michelle.

You all watch TV in the family room. No one speaks. When the Bellers get home, Michelle and Nicole immediately show them the broken things. Mr. Beller yells, "What were you doing in here?"

Nicole says, sobbing, "We were dancing. There's more room in here." She doesn't mention the drinking.

You say, "It's my fault. I fell and bumped into the case. I'll pay you for everything that got broken."

Mrs. Beller says, "These things can't be replaced. Not for any amount of money."

She picks up the broken pieces. "I'll see about having them fixed. But they won't be as valuable."

Katherine says, "We'll all help pay."

"Thank you, dear," Mrs. Beller smiles weakly at Katherine. "After I get an estimate, we can talk."

Mr. Beller takes you home. You're afraid he will tell your parents, but he drops you off in front of the house.

The next day at school, you ask Nicole what her parents are going to do. She says, "I don't know except they grounded us for a month."

"How are we going to do the science project?" you ask.

"I'll talk to them about it tonight."

Turn to page 33.

That evening, Nicole calls you. "Let's work on **33** the project after school tomorrow."

Your mother gives you permission. You feel bad about going back to Nicole's house.

The next day, you and Nicole and Katherine work on the science project. Michelle stays downstairs with you. When the Bellers get home, Mrs. Beller says, "I took the broken porcelain to a shop today. I can get a new vase just like the broken one. But the figurines aren't available anymore. They said they can fix them, though. Here's the estimate of what it will cost." She hands a sheet of paper to Michelle, who passes it around.

When you see the numbers, you are shocked. You can never earn that much money!

"We've decided all four of you should share equally in the cost," Mrs. Beller says, "even though Jamie actually fell on the glass case.

"Michelle and Nicole will work at our store to pay their share. Katherine and Jamie, you can either work in the store, or you can let your parents decide how you'll pay it off."

Katherine says, "Please don't tell my mother. She gets so upset. I'll work in your store."

They look at you.

If you decide to work in the Bellers' store,
turn to page 57.
If you tell your parents and have them decide how
you will pay for your damage, turn to page 59.

After dinner, Steve goes to his room to study. **35** You follow him and tell him what happened. "How can I get out of the assignment?" you ask.

Steve asks, "Did your teacher assign you to work with them?"

"Yes, I thought it would be fun. I didn't know something like this would happen. I'll feel funny around them now."

"Your choices are to keep working with them, or to ask your teacher to let you do a different assignment. If you want to keep working with the girls, you can tell them how you feel about drinking. You could work here instead of at Nicole's house. Mom is always home after school and nothing bad could happen. Or you could explain to your teacher that you don't want to work with them."

If you decide to talk to the girls, turn to page 55.
If you decide to talk to your teacher,
turn to page 37.

Early the next day, you catch Mr. Burke alone in the classroom. "I can't work with Nicole and Katherine on the science project."

Mr. Burke frowns. "Are they excluding you from the project?"

"Not exactly. I just, um, think they're not serious about it. I want to get a good grade."

"Would you like to meet with me and both of them to discuss it?"

"No!" you say. If the teacher makes you all talk about it, the others might think you told about the drinking. "Can't you just let me do another assignment?"

Mr. Burke looks at you like he knows there's something you're not telling him. He says, "I'll let you know this afternoon."

Turn to page 39.

When school starts, Nicole tells you Katherine is **39** at home sick. Nicole doesn't feel well, either. She asks if you are coming over to work on the project after school.

You say, "I don't know."

As you leave for recess, Mr. Burke says, "Nicole and Jamie, will you stay for a few minutes, please."

"What's wrong with Katherine today?"

"She's sick," says Nicole. "I think she has the flu."

"Is there any connection between her illness and Jamie telling me this morning that she doesn't want to work with the two of you on the science project?"

Nicole looks at you with surprise and anger.

"No," you say. "I didn't even know she was sick. It's just what I told you."

Nicole turns to Mr. Burke. "We don't want to work with her, either. So, you can just give us different assignments."

The teacher looks at both of you sadly. "So, there's no way you can work together?"

Turn to page 41.

"I guess not," you answer. You feel miserable. **41** Nicole is angry at you, and you feel like you betrayed her.

"All right, I'll give you separate assignments," he says.

As you walk out to the playground, you tell Nicole, "I'm sorry I didn't talk to you first. But I didn't like the drinking at your house yesterday."

"Did you think we drink all the time? It was the first time we ever tried it. The last, too! I felt really sick last night. Katherine threw up and has a hangover today. But you didn't even wait to talk to us. I guess you are just so perfect you can't put up with anybody who makes a mistake." She walks away rapidly, and joins a group of her friends. She acts like she's forgotten all about you.

Turn to page 43.

You realize you have lost your chance for friendship with Nicole. You had assumed she was acting like her usual self yesterday.

Your friend Kelli beckons for you to join her. "I thought you'd want to play with Nicole and her friends since you are working on the science project together."

"We aren't working together anymore."

"What happened?" Kelli asks.

You say, "It didn't work out after all." But all the while you talk to her, you think about how you can apologize to Nicole.

At lunch, you write a note to Nicole and leave it on her desk:

> I don't think I'm perfect. I made a big mistake not talking to you before I talked to Mr. Burke. I hope you can forgive me.

When she comes back Nicole reads the note. She looks at you and nods. You feel better.

The End

She waits for an answer. **45**

You say, "I was scared to tell you. The first time I went to Nicole's house, her sister stayed up in her room. Nicole got into her parents' liquor. We all drank some. It made me fall asleep. We burned a pizza and made a big mess. We didn't drink anymore after that."

Your mother says, "I'm disappointed that you didn't feel you could tell me."

"I knew you'd be upset. I didn't know how to tell them I didn't want to drink. I wanted to be friends."

"That worries me more than anything, Jamie. You knew the difference between right and wrong. You still did the wrong thing because the others wanted you to. You can get in a lot worse trouble if you don't learn to say 'no' to something you know is wrong and that you don't want to do."

"I know, Mom. But I don't want Nicole and Katherine for friends anymore. I have a weird feeling when I'm around them. I'll never do anything like that again."

Your mom gives you a hug and says, "I'm proud you discovered that on your own."

The End

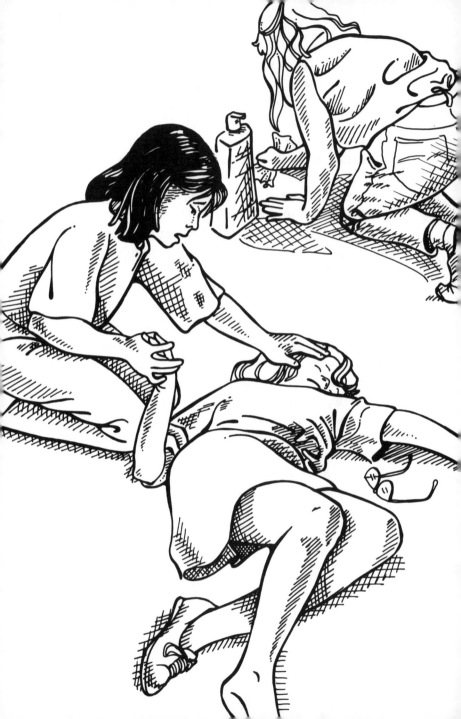

It's awful being ignored. If you drink with **47** Katherine and Nicole, they might be more friendly. You hold out your glass. "Give me some, too."

The stuff tastes awful! You choke, then laugh, and the girls laugh with you. You don't drink anymore; you just leave some alcohol in your glass and pretend. The others don't even notice.

All of a sudden Katherine's face goes white and she jumps up. She staggers a few steps and falls down. She throws up on the carpet and then faints. You and Nicole can't wake her up.

Nicole seems more worried about the carpet. "Help me clean up."

"What about Katherine?"

"She's just sleeping it off. But my parents will kill me if they see this mess."

You help Nicole clean the carpet, even though it's gross. But you worry about Katherine. While Nicole erases the evidence, you try to waken Katherine.

"Leave her alone," says Nicole. "She's okay."

You have never felt more scared in your life. Katherine looks strange. She takes short, shallow breaths and her face is colorless. You run upstairs and knock on Michelle's door. Michelle opens her door. "What is it?" She looks cross.

"Katherine fainted."

"Geez, can't you kids manage not to get into trouble?"

"What a smell! What happened?"

Turn to page 49.

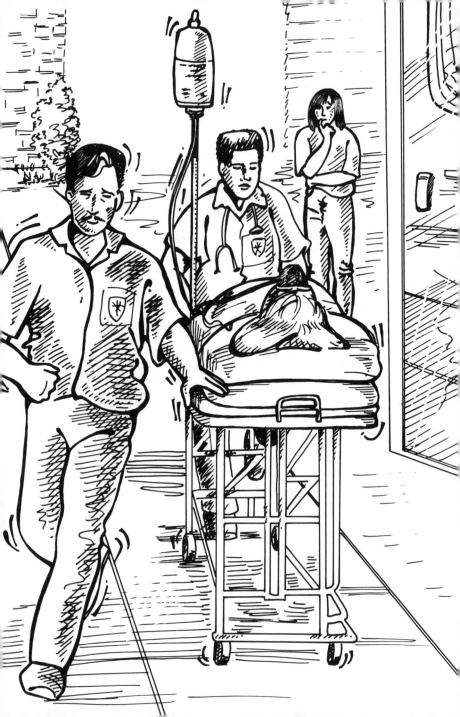

Nicole says, "Katherine threw up and then she went to sleep. Maybe she's got the flu or something." She doesn't mention alcohol.

"Let's get her onto the couch." Michelle motions for you and Nicole to help lift Katherine. "We'll let her sleep until Mom and Dad come home."

You decide that you better do something. If you dial 9-1-1, the person who answers might tell you what to do. You go to the kitchen phone.

A woman's voice answers, "Is this an emergency?"

"I'm not sure," you say, even more scared now. You almost hang up, but the woman starts to talk to you in a calm way.

She asks if Katherine is breathing, and you tell her, "Yes, but her breathing is kind of funny." She says she'll send an aid unit. You hang up, relieved.

When the sisters find out you called 9-1-1, they are angry. "We'll get in trouble," Nicole says.

They don't seem to care about Katherine, and you decide they are selfish.

The ambulence arrives. An aide radios headquarters to notify Katherine's mother and have her meet them at the hospital. They put Katherine on a stretcher and carry her out.

Michelle and Nicole look scared. Michelle asks, "Is there really something wrong with her?"

"She's in serious condition," says the paramedic.

The ambulence drives off, siren wailing. You call your mother and tell her what happened.

Turn to page 51.

It's later in the evening when you finally are allowed to go to the hospital. Katherine is pale and tired. "I had to have a tube put up my nose and down my throat to have my stomach pumped out. It was awful. They said I could have died."

An older woman comes in the room. "Are you the girl who was with Katherine when she got sick?"

"Yes," you answer.

"I told Katherine to stay away from you. She and Nicole have never done anything like this. You got the girls into trouble. Get out of here."

You start to cry and run out of the room. Through your tears you tell your mother what Katherine's mother said. "It wasn't my fault they were drinking, honestly."

"I know, dear. You aren't to blame for Katherine and Nicole drinking. But you are responsible for your own drinking. Still, I'm proud that you were brave enough to call for help."

"I'm sorry I drank. I didn't want to, but I wanted to be their friend. Mom, what should I do about the science project? I can't work with them anymore."

"I'll talk to your teacher tomorrow. We'll arrange something else for you. You've had a tough lesson, but I think you've learned from it. Just remember alcohol is a poison. If you drink too much, it can kill you."

"I'll remember. This was the worst day of my life."

The End

You don't want to act that silly, so you decide not to drink. When you have finished the pizza, you say, "Let's start on the science project." They laugh uproariously.

"Come on. That's the reason for getting together." You open up your book. "To do the 'Generating Electricity' experiment, we need wire, tape, a block of wood and thumbtacks, a compass, and a horseshoe magnet."

Nicole and Katherine giggle over your instructions and make silly comments, but after a while join in the plans. Nicole puts away the bottles and gets some soda to drink. She says she'll ask her dad to get the things you need. You can all work on making your generator tomorrow after school.

The next day your best friend Kelli asks how your project is going. You say it is okay, but you hope next time you and she can work together. You make plans for her to spend a weekend night with you.

After school you go back to Nicole's house to finish the project. Nicole and Katherine don't drink again; instead they watch soap operas and giggle over the plots. You end up doing most of the assignment by yourself. You're glad you won't need to spend anymore time with the girls.

The End

You decide to tell the other girls you don't want to work with them.

The next day, Nicole says Katherine is absent because she got sick from drinking. She asks if you are coming over.

You had planned to tell both girls together that you can't work with them anymore. You decide you had better talk with Nicole now. "I felt bad about drinking yesterday. My mom would be mad if she found out. I don't want to do it anymore. If you're going to keep on drinking, it would be better if we ask Mr. Burke if we can do our own projects."

"That's okay. Katherine already told me she isn't going to drink anymore. I don't want to either."

You call your mother for permission to go to Nicole's. Katherine comes over too, although she is pale and has a headache.

At first you feel embarrassed with the other girls, but the awkwardness goes away.

You get a B+ on the assignment. You're not sure if you still want to be friends with Nicole and Katherine. When your mom says you can have a slumber party for your birthday, you decide to invite them, as well as your best friend Kelli. At the party, everyone has a good time. You're glad you can be friends.

The End

You know your parents would be upset and disappointed, but if you work in the Bellers' store, you could pay for the damage without them finding out.

The Bellers own a grocery store. You will stock shelves and help customers after school on different days until the damage is paid for.

You tell your parents you are working on a special project for school with Nicole and Katherine. They allow you to go to Nicole's house on Mondays and Thursdays after school.

You sort of enjoy working in the store. But you worry about your parents finding out you lied. It would be worse if they found out you were drinking and damaged the Bellers' property.

One day, your mother comes into the store. By the look on her face, you can see you are in trouble.

"I tried to call you at the Bellers'," she says. "What is going on here?"

Mrs. Beller comes up and says, "Jamie is working here to pay for some damage she did at our house. Didn't she tell you?"

Your mother looks surprised and angry.

"I was embarrassed," you say. "Can I tell you at home later?"

Mrs. Beller says, "It's almost closing time. Why don't you go with your mother now?"

Turn to page 59.

When you finish telling her about it, your mom says, "Jamie, I'm very disappointed in you, and not just because of what you did at the Bellers'. Although I'm unhappy that you were drinking, it looks like you have learned your lesson, and you're paying the Bellers back. But the worst thing was lying to your dad and me. You are going to have to work very hard to regain our trust."

The next day, after school, your mother says, "Your dad and I talked it over last night. You can continue your piano lessons and Camp Fire, because I know you have supervision there. And you can continue to work at the Bellers' store until you've paid off your obligation. But you are not to go anywhere on weekends or any other time unless one of us is along. After you are through working at the Bellers', we will talk about it again and see what you have learned."

You are upset that you can't go to your friends' houses or do any fun things. But seeing the hurt in your mother's eyes and knowing you let her down makes you feel worst of all. You decide from now on you will be more honest about your problems.

The End

The Decision Is Yours Series

These enjoyable books help children ages 7-11 years think about social problems. Written in a "choose-your-own-ending" format, the child decides what action the character will take.

$5.95 each, paperback, 64 pages, illustrated
$16.95 each, library binding

Finders, Keepers?
by Elizabeth Crary
What do you do when a friend wants the money from a wallet you found?

Bully on the Bus
by Carl Bosch
What do you do when Nick, a kid bigger than you, wants to beat you up?

Making the Grade
by Carl Bosch
Help Jennifer decide what to do about a bad report card when she has spent more time on the soccer field than on her homework.

First Day Blues
by Peggy King Anderson
It's your first day in a new school. How will you make friends?

Under Whose Influence?
by Judy Laik
Help Jamie decide whether or not to drink alcohol with her friends.

Leader's Guide for The Decision Is Yours Series
by Carl Bosch
Spiralbound guide to activities just right for exploring values, problem solving, peer pressure, ethics, feelings, and more with elementary and middle-school classes.
$14.95

Order these books from Parenting Press, Inc. by calling
1-800-992-6657. Visa & MasterCard accepted. Mention Dept. 402.
Complete book catalog available on request.

(Prices subject to change without notice.)